The Hemingway Tradition

The Hemingway Tradition

Kristin Butcher

Orca

ORCA BOOK PUBLISHERS

Library and Archives Canada Cataloguing in Publication
Butcher, Kristin
The Hemingway tradition

(Orca soundings)
ISBN 10: 1-55143-242-0 ISBN 13: 978-1-55143-242-7

I. Title. II. Series.

PS8553.U6972H45 2002   jC813'.54   C2002-910696-6
PZ7.B9691He 2002

Summary: After his father commits suicide, Shaw struggles to
come to terms with the death and move on.

First published in the United States, 2002
Library of Congress Control Number: 2002107488

Orca Book Publishers gratefully acknowledges the support for its publishing programs provided by the following agencies: the Government of
Canada through the Book Publishing Industry Development Program and
the Canada Council for the Arts, and the Province of British Columbia
through the BC Arts Council and the Book Publishing Tax Credit.

Cover design by Teresa Bubela
Cover photography by Eyewire

ORCA BOOK PUBLISHERS   ORCA BOOK PUBLISHERS
PO Box 5626, STN. B   PO Box 468
VICTORIA, BC CANADA   CUSTER, WA USA
V8R 6S4   98240-0468

www.orcabook.com
Printed and bound in Canada.
Printed on 100% PCW recycled paper.
12 11 10 09 • 7 6 5 4

Chapter One

We had the top down on our old LeBaron and the sun was beating on us from a sky that was nothing but blue. It was my mom's turn to drive. I was stretched out in the passenger seat, watching Saskatchewan slide by and thinking there must be a couple dozen different ways for a guy to kill himself.

Hanging was the first thing that popped into my head. It's so convenient. You can do it almost anywhere with almost anything. A telephone cord, belt, bed sheet. Whatever's handy. And depending on how much effort you want to put into it, you can break your neck and die instantly or dangle for a while until you suffocate. The cowboys in the Old West had the best idea, though. They just threw a rope over the branch of a tall tree, slipped the noose around the neck of the hangee—usually a cattle rustler—and then whacked the rump of his horse so it took off without him. *Slam, bam, rest in peace, Sam.*

Very effective, but not for everybody. Another popular suicide method is wrist slitting.

But that's way too much blood for me. Of course, walking in front of a bus or diving off a bridge would work too. But I'd want something a little less traumatic. Something like poison maybe, or carbon monoxide, or sleeping pills. Something where you just slip away without realizing you're going. I know that makes me seem like a chicken, but I think that's because I don't want to die. If I did I might have a whole different take on things. I might even do what my dad did.

He ate a bullet and blew half his head away. Messy, but it did the job. I ought to know. I'm the one who found him.

The memory of that afternoon flared inside my head like a match struck in the dark. I flinched. I couldn't help it. Though it had been months already, my nerves were still raw.

My dad would've been proud.

"Explore your feelings! Sharpen your senses! Harness your emotions to breathe life into your writing!" That's what he was always telling me. Sometimes he'd get right into my face as he was saying it. I could see the sparks fly from his eyes. I was certain that if they landed on me, I would start to burn with the same fire that was in him.

I turned to look at the memory that was chasing me. Okay. So how would Dad have described it in one of his books?

Dylan Sebring, so considerate of others during life, was less so in death. Oh, he'd written a farewell note. And he'd even covered the bed with heavy plastic before lying on it. But the plastic was no defense against the force of a .45-caliber bullet. His brains were part of the wallpaper before Dylan finished squeezing the trigger. The flies found him first. Then his son. By that time the day had warmed up—after all, it was June. Afterwards, Shaw couldn't remember whether it was the stench of death or the sight of his father in a million sticky pieces that made his stomach heave.

"Hey, Sleeping Beauty." Mom's voice cut through the wind rumbling around my ears. "Wake up. It's your turn to drive."

She slowed down and eased the car over to the side of the highway. I pushed myself up in the seat and stretched.

"We'll drive as far as Regina and then call it a day," she said, slipping the car into park. "I'd say another forty minutes and we should be there."

I stepped onto the pavement, yawned and looked around. I decided Saskatchewan had to be the most boring province in all of Canada. Traveling across it was like running on a treadmill. You never seemed to get anywhere.

It was just mile after flat mile of blue flax, yellow sunflowers and waist-high wheat. There weren't even any curves in the road to jazz things up. You could practically drive all the way from Alberta to Manitoba without ever touching the steering wheel.

I adjusted the seat and mirror, fastened my seatbelt, stepped on the gas and headed back onto #1 East. Then I grabbed a CD, slipped it into the player and cranked it up. I'd burned it especially for the trip. Stuff I liked, but tame enough that my mom wouldn't nag me about my taste in music.

So there we were, cruising along the highway, listening to tunes. Mom's arm was stretched out along the back of the seat. I could feel her fingers tapping out the beat on the upholstery. I glanced over at her. She looked back and grinned, then squeezed my neck.

From behind us a horn blared. A silver SUV pulled up alongside. Its radio was so loud I could feel the bass inside my clothes.

There was a gang of university-age guys leaning out the windows, hooting and hollering and grinning like idiots. The SUV was staying even with us, and I tightened my grip on the steering wheel. For a second, I thought they wanted to drag. Then they gave me a big thumbs up, leaned on the horn again and took off.

I slapped the steering wheel and started to split a gut.

Mom turned the music down. "What was all that about?" And then as she realized I was laughing, she said, "And what's so funny?"

Still smirking, I nodded toward the SUV pulling away. "Those guys. They thought you were hitting on me." Then I started to laugh again.

"Hitting on you? Get out!" she said, but she was smiling now too. "Why would I hit on you? I'm old enough to be your mother."

I sent her a sideways glance. "You are my mother."

Her grin got bigger. "There you go. What did I tell you!"

"But I can see how those guys might have gotten the wrong idea," I teased. "As far as moms go, you're okay."

She made a face. "Well, thank you very much. I think." Then she ran her hand through her windblown hair and sighed. "Maybe there's hope for me yet. I'll get myself a slinky little dress and start prowling the bars for a boy toy. I can be one of those cheetahs you told me about."

That set me howling again.

"You mean cougar," I corrected her.

"Cheetah, cougar, whatever." She smiled good-naturedly. "I knew it was some kind of cat." Then she started to giggle. For a second she almost looked like a teenager. "Can't you just see me? God, I haven't been into a bar in years!

I wouldn't know what to do. Those places are for single people, not old married ladies like me."

I wanted to tell her *"You're not married anymore,"* but there was no point. Dad had already squeezed into the front seat between us.

Chapter Two

And here I was, hoping we'd left him behind in Vancouver. I should've known it wouldn't be that easy.

My dad had been one of Canada's better-known writers. Even without the dramatic exit, his death would've made the six o'clock news. And because I was his son, as well as the one who discovered his body, I was news too. Neighbors, teachers, kids at school, suddenly it seemed like everybody was staring at me. From a distance, of course, as if suicide was contagious.

Like maybe if they got too close, they'd suddenly feel the need to throw themselves under a truck. I hate to think how they would've acted if they'd known about the note.

But they didn't.

Mom and I kept that to ourselves. The police would call it withholding evidence. We saw it as protecting a trust. We never talked about keeping it a secret. We both just knew that's what we had to do.

The worst was the house, though. Even after it had been cleaned up and not so much as a molecule of my dad was left, he was still there. I could feel him everywhere.

I think it must've been the same for Mom. She never slept in their bedroom again. And then at the end of July, she said we were moving.

My mom's an actuary for a big insurance company, and she told me she'd been transferred to Winnipeg. She made it sound like it was the company's idea, but I wasn't fooled.

The timing was a little too convenient. Besides, my grandparents live in Winnipeg, and that's where my mom grew up. I never told her I didn't believe her, though. Pretending was easier for both of us.

The next thing I knew, it was time to head back to school. I couldn't believe it. It was only August 29! In Vancouver, school never started until after Labor Day, so I was getting gypped out of almost a week's vacation. But when I stopped to think about it, I was sort of glad. Since my mom had started her new job, I'd spent so much time alone I was starting to talk to myself. I was ready to meet some new people.

That first day was pretty much like it had been at my old school. But because everything was new and strange and I didn't know anybody, it felt totally different. Normally I would've tracked down my friends and hung out with them until the bell rang. But because I didn't have any friends, I just leaned against the school, trying not to look out of place.

Dakota Collegiate Institute—DCI for short—was smaller than my old school, but not by much. It sat on a corner close to a busy intersection, so kids were coming at it from every direction. There were transit stops on both sides of the street, and every few minutes a bus would dump a fresh batch of bodies onto the sidewalk. Other kids arrived on foot, skateboard and bicycle, and the rest came by car, rumbling into the gravel parking lot with their radios blasting. By the time the bell rang, the place was so jammed it looked and sounded like a massive outdoor concert. The way everyone pushed into the building, you would've thought they were giving money away inside. Not that I'm criticizing—I was part of the herd too.

"Ow!" a girl beside me grumbled. "Walk much?"

"Sorry," I apologized, quickly picking up my size thirteen foot. But when I put it back down, I could tell by the lump under it that I was standing on something other than pavement again.

"For crying out loud!" the girl complained and gave me a shove. "Could you try walking on your own feet instead of mine?"

"Sorry," I apologized for the second time in less than a minute. Then I tried a joke. "There seems to be a sidewalk shortage." I grinned down at her hopefully. She was pretty short, and next to me, she looked even shorter. Even though I wouldn't be seventeen until January, I was already six-foot-two.

She rolled her eyes and turned back to the girl beside her.

So much for humor. I was obviously going to have to stop stepping on toes if I hoped to make any friends.

I'd had a tour of the school when I registered, so I found my homeroom without much trouble—not that it did me any good. All the seats were taken by the time I got there. Some guy snagged the last desk by the door just as I arrived. The only other empty chair was at the very front of the class. Great. Now I was not only the new kid, I was also a geek. The day just kept getting better and better.

"Locker 131—Jai Dhillon and Shaw Sebring." The teacher glanced up from the paper in front of her and peered around the room.

I looked around too, just in time to see this little East Indian kid jump out of his seat like he'd been popped out of a toaster—flashing the biggest smile I'd ever seen outside a beauty pageant. Right away everyone else in the room grinned too.

"Go, Jai-i! Go, Jai-i!" someone chanted, and the other kids started to clap.

It was pretty clear my locker partner was either the class clown or a leader of the people.

But at that moment all I cared about was that I wasn't going to have any competition for the top shelf of our locker.

"I don't remember you from Grade 10," Jai said, as we taped our timetables to the inside of the door. "Were you here last year?"

I shook my head. "No. I just moved to Winnipeg a week ago."

"Oh, yeah? From where?"

"Vancouver."

"Vancouver!" Jai looked at me as if I was crazy. "Why the heck would you trade Vancouver for Winnipeg? We get winter here you know, like nine months of the year!"

I shrugged. "My mom's company transferred her."

"Ahhh," Jai nodded knowingly, and then out of the blue he asked, "How tall are you?"

"Six-two."

"You play volleyball?"

I did, but I wanted to know where Jai was going with all his questions before I committed myself. I frowned. "Why do you want to know?"

He flashed his huge grin. "Because we could use you on the team. Tryouts start tonight at eight o'clock."

"You play volleyball?" I said in amazement. I tried to picture Jai smashing a ball. "No offense, but you're kind of short, aren't you?"

He flexed his fingers and, if possible, the grin got bigger. "Not for a setter."

The bell rang and we both squinted at our timetables.

"English—second floor," I mumbled, pulling a map of the school out of my jeans.

"I got math," Jai said, "and I'm on the second floor too. Come on. I'll show you the way."

This time I got to the room before it completely filled up. Jai poked his head in and looked around. After a couple of seconds, he elbowed me in the ribs and started zigzagging around desks and people.

"Come on," he called back. "I'll introduce you to a friend of mine."

From the way he grinned at everyone he passed, I figured that could've been anybody in the school.

"Tess," he said to a girl standing with her back to us. "I want you to meet a new friend of mine—Shaw Sebring. Shaw, this is Tess Petersen."

The girl spun around. "Hi." She looked up at me and smiled. Then the smile slid from her mouth and her glance shifted to my feet. She took a step back and turned to Jai. "We've met."

Chapter Three

I took the seat behind Tess. Despite the fact that the two of us had literally gotten off on the wrong foot, we were soon gabbing like old friends.

When her face wasn't screwed up in pain, Tess was actually kind of pretty. I think it was her eyes. They were icy blue, and they danced. I know that sounds corny, but it's true. I've never seen anyone with eyes like that. They didn't sit still for a second, and when they looked at you, it was more like they were looking into you. In a way it was kind of creepy. I kept wondering if Tess was learning more about me than I wanted her to.

Of course, I was finding out stuff about her too—like how tall she was. Or maybe I should say, how short she was—five-foot-one and three-quarters according to her. Her dad was a mechanic and her mom managed a flower shop. She had two older brothers, a cat named Hercules, and a dog named Gertie. Tess said she was originally from Nova Scotia, but her family had moved to Winnipeg when she was ten. She didn't play sports, but she was a true-blue Dakota fan and hardly ever missed a game. Otherwise, she spent most of her time working on the school paper. From the way her face lit up when she told me that, I could tell it was important to her. She invited me to join too, but luckily the teacher started the class before Tess could corner me for an answer.

In most subjects, the only thing you do on the first day is get textbooks and course outlines. But in English, there's almost always that What I did on my Summer Vacation essay. Miss Boswell put a slightly different spin on it, but it amounted to the same thing, and the truth is I didn't want to think about the summer, never mind write about it.

The entire class groaned at the prospect of doing work. But because it was the first day and we were still on our best behavior, we settled down pretty quick. Soon the room was quiet. The only sound was thirty pens scratching on paper. Okay, I lied. Twenty-nine pens. Mine was twirling on my fingers.

"Welcome to Dakota," a voice whispered in my ear. My pen suddenly jumped out of my hand and clattered to the floor.

"Thanks," I mumbled self-consciously, leaning over to pick it up. Then I frowned at the empty paper in front of me. It didn't contain so much as a doodle. I braced myself for teacher lecture #107 on wasting time. But it didn't come. In fact, Miss Boswell didn't even seem to notice my paper.

And as soon as the next sentence left her mouth, I knew why.

"So you're Dylan Sebring's son."

I didn't say anything. I didn't even nod. But that didn't stop Miss Boswell.

"I'm a big fan of your father's work," she said. "I've read every book he's ever written—many times. He's one of the best suspense writers this country has ever produced. You must be very proud."

I stared at her in disbelief. Proud? That wasn't exactly the word that came to mind. Hurt, humiliated, angry and confused maybe. But certainly not proud.

A couple of the kids nearby had stopped writing. I could feel their eyes drilling into me. Any second now, Miss Boswell was going to say something about my dad's suicide, and then I'd be a freak all over again. I willed her to stop talking but the vibes didn't reach her. She kept on going.

"From your school records, it would seem you've inherited your father's gift. According to your last English teacher, you're extremely talented." Miss Boswell put a hand on my shoulder. "I look forward to reading your work."

Then she smiled and continued her tour of the classroom. And that was that.

At least it was until Tess swiveled around in her seat.

"Your dad's a famous writer?" she croaked, barely able to keep her voice to a whisper. Then without waiting for me to answer, she demanded, "Why didn't you tell me? This is great! Now for sure you've got to join the newspaper club. We could interview your dad and do a super fantastic article. Maybe even a series. Hey, wait a minute! I've got a better idea. Your dad could come and talk to us—you know, explain the ins and outs of the publishing industry. That would get everybody so inspired. Do you think he would do it?"

"No," I said bluntly, avoiding Tess's eyes and focusing instead on dating my paper. I was pressing so hard it was more like an engraving than writing.

"How can you say that?" Tess sounded offended. "You haven't even asked him."

Miss Boswell shot us a get-to-work glance, and Tess reluctantly turned around. But as soon as Miss Boswell looked away, she was back again.

"How do you know he wouldn't do it?" she pressed.

"Because."

"Because why?"

I blurted the first thing that popped into my head. "Because he's not writing anymore."

It was the truth—as far as it went.

Tess's gasp made me look up, and right away I felt myself being cross-examined by her eyes.

"He quit?" she squeaked.

"You could say that." I frowned and tried to look away. All I wanted was a little privacy. Why couldn't Tess turn around and mind her own business?

"Why would he do that?" she said.

"Could we talk about this some other time?" I turned back to my paper, hoping she'd take the hint, but the journalist in her was too strong. She started firing questions at me, and with each one I felt more and more cornered.

"Why would your dad stop doing something he's good at? Did he get another job? Did he run out of ideas? Did he get terminal writer's block? Did he get so rich that he just decided to retire? Did he… "

Something inside me exploded.

"He died! Okay?" I growled into her face. "He put a gun into his mouth, and he pulled the trigger. That's why he isn't writing anymore, and that's why he's not going to come and talk to your news-paper club. So could we please drop the subject?"

I looked up, expecting to see the entire class staring at me. Everyone was still hard at work. I was sure I'd been yelling, but the only one who seemed to have heard me was Tess.

I looked back at her. Her eyes had stopped dancing.

"Yeah, sure," she mumbled and turned around in her seat.

Chapter Four

I dug the ball up, then tore around the net and dove to retrieve my own bump. My hip bones cracked as they collided with the hardwood. I knew my bruise count had risen again.

"Where the heck does Mr. Hudson get these killer drills?" I asked Jai as we gulped water from the fountain during a timeout.

He wiped his mouth with the back of his hand and shrugged. "A million years of coaching volleyball would be my guess. But you can't argue with success." He pointed to the banners hung high around the gym wall. "Dakota's volleyball team has a habit of winning. In the last ten or twelve provincial tournaments, we've gone all the way to the final four—or farther. It doesn't seem to matter who's on the team. Once Mr. Hudson gets hold of them, they turn into volleyball players."

"Or they die trying," I grumbled. I examined a welt on my forearm.

"You're just out of shape, you wimp," Jai teased. "You should be happy you made the team."

I was happy. During the two weeks of tryouts I'd become totally wrapped up in the sport. Not only did it push me physically, it was also a good way to meet people. But most important of all, it kept my mind occupied.

After practice, a bunch of us leaned against the bleachers while Mr. Hudson gave us pointers on how not to shank the ball.

"It'll come. It just takes practice." The comment was harmless, but the gleeful little half-smile that went with it wasn't. I instantly had visions of more torturous drills. Mr. Hudson headed across the gym to his office. "See you fellas Wednesday."

"Yeah. See ya," we replied, pushing ourselves away from the bleachers and starting for the exit. Then the guy in front of me stopped.

"Darn! I forgot my hat," he groaned, doing a quick about-face and jogging back to the change room.

I reached into my jacket pocket for my car keys.

"Hey, Brian," I yelled after him, "while you're in there, tell Jai to hurry up. I want to get going." Jai's house was between my apartment and the school, so I usually gave him a ride to practice.

Brian pushed open the change-room door. As he disappeared inside, I heard him holler, "Hey, Dhillon, you homo. Hustle your ass or your date is going to leave without you."

It was the sort of smart-ass comment guys are always making to one another. It didn't mean anything. I knew that. But it bugged me just the same. As I headed to the parking lot, the adrenaline that had been racing through my veins from two hours of physical activity began to evaporate. By the time I got home, it had disappeared altogether. When my mom spoke to me, I realized I was in a lousy mood.

"How was practice?"

I dropped my sports bag onto the floor and shrugged off my jacket. "It was okay." Then I headed for the kitchen.

"Don't leave that there, Shaw." Mom pointed to my bag. "One of us will trip over it. Put it away."

"Can I get in the door first?" I snapped back. Even I could hear the attitude in my voice, but surprisingly, my mom didn't get on my case. She just gave me a dirty look and turned back to the television.

I opened the fridge and peered inside. I wasn't really hungry, but checking out the contents of the fridge was something I had to do. Call it force of habit. And since I was there, I figured I might as well make it worth my while. I took a swig of milk from the carton and grabbed an apple. Then I picked up my gear and started for my room.

My intention was to hole up in there for the rest of the night, but Mom stopped me before I could escape. She gestured to my schoolbooks spread out on the dining-room table. I figured she was trying to tell me to put them away too.

She wasn't.

"I see you got an English essay back," she said. "The mark's not too impressive."

I instantly saw fire. "What are you doing poking through my stuff?" I demanded.

Mom raised an eyebrow. "Well, aren't you Mr. Congeniality? I wasn't snooping through your things. It was sitting on the table in full view. If you didn't want me to see it, maybe you should have put it away. The point is, it's not very good. You were lucky to get a C."

"What's the matter with a C? There are a lot of kids who would give their eyeteeth to get a C on an essay."

"I'm sure there are, but you're not one of them. You wrote better than that when you were in Grade 4. So what's the big idea?"

"I didn't like the topic." I scowled.

Mom tossed the remote control onto the coffee table. "Since when has that ever mattered? You've had some pretty bizarre assignments over the years, Shaw, but you've always managed to turn them into something interesting." She paused. "That's because you're a writer."

"No!" The word leaped into the air between us. "You've got the wrong Sebring! Dad was the one who was the writer!"

"Then it would stand to reason that's where you get it from, don't you think?" Mom replied calmly. "Your father was a writer. So are you."

I shook my head fiercely. "No!" I said again. "You're wrong. I'm not a writer. Dad just wanted me to be one."

Mom frowned and sat forward on the couch. "Shaw, you're not making any sense. You love writing. From the time you were old enough to know what books were, you've been making up stories. I can't remember when you wanted to be anything but an author like your dad. You have no idea how thrilled he was about that. And how proud. He couldn't wait for you to grow up so that the two of you could write the novel to end all novels. Don't you remember? You used to sit with your heads together for hours planning it."

The vision of my dad as I'd last seen him flashed into my brain in brilliant, gory detail. For some reason, the memory didn't seem to know it was supposed to fade. I winced. And then suddenly I started to tremble, as if an earthquake had started up deep inside me and was working its way to the surface.

Already my knees felt weak, and my hands were starting to sweat.

I picked up my bag and threw my mom a parting glare. "Well, in case you haven't noticed, the plan has changed," I snarled.

Then I stomped off to my room.

Chapter Five

One minute you're standing on solid ground; the next—you're falling. Write about the experience.

I shook my head. Where did Miss Boswell dig up these lame writing themes?

I glanced at the clock. It was ten to eight. Mom would be back from her dinner meeting in an hour. I wanted to have the assignment out of the way before then. Otherwise she'd ask to see it. After our run-in the other night, I wasn't all that anxious to share.

I took a deep breath and read the theme again—out loud. It didn't help. The topic was still awful. I tried to think of some story possibilities anyway. Avalanche? Trap door in a floor? Earthquake? Falling off a cliff? Yeah, right. Like every kid in the class wasn't going to write about those things.

What do you care? I argued with myself.

As long as I completed the assignment and got a passing grade, it shouldn't matter what I wrote. Of course, thinking that and actually believing it weren't quite the same thing. My father had trained me better than I realized.

It was kind of ironic how that had worked out. While my dad was alive, I'd wanted to be just like him. But since his death, I was working all the time to prove we were entirely different.

To anyone besides me, and maybe my mom, that would probably seem really dumb. After all, my dad was a great guy. Everyone liked him. He was smart, passionate about his work and family, and he loved life.

At least I always thought he loved life. But according to the note he left, he'd had problems that were too big to handle. Problems I hadn't known anything about.

Woooff! Like a gasoline explosion, the blistering vision of his death began to burn the back of my eyes. I squeezed them shut, trying to extinguish the fire.

Why wouldn't that memory leave me alone?

"Go away!" I growled through clenched teeth.

And then, as if all I'd had to do was ask, the blood-soaked bedroom began to dissolve. It slid down the walls of my mind as if it were being hosed into a storm sewer. I watched with fascination. I felt the tension in my body drain away with the dirty water.

Gradually I became aware of a gentle rocking. And then the lazy lapping of waves on the hull of a small boat. My body melted deeper into the molded seat of the runabout and I squinted at the sunlight winking on the water. Dad, wearing the old, threadbare sweater he kept strictly for fishing, was stretched out on the seat across from me with his feet propped on the gunwale. His eyes were closed, and his long, lean body was swaying with the rhythm of the boat. His fishing rod lay across his lap, its line dangling idly in the water, slack and then taut as the current tugged on it. My line was hanging out the other side of the boat. But Dad and I weren't really fishing. In fact, we hadn't checked our bait in over an hour. It was enough that we were sharing the morning in that secluded cove.

After a while Dad sighed, and without opening his eyes, he said, "I wonder if it was times like this that inspired Ernest Hemingway to write *The Old Man and the Sea*. That book was really something. Almost the entire story was set in a tiny boat with just one character—two if you count the fish. Must've made dialogue a bit of a challenge." He opened one eye to see if I was listening.

Then satisfied that he had my attention, he shut it again and went on talking. "He was quite the outdoorsman, Hemingway was. Learned to fish in the rivers and lakes of Michigan with his dad." He opened his eye again and smiled lazily. "Kind of like you and me."

I put the memory on pause and stepped back to look at it. It was so real.

I felt like I was living that morning all over again. Part of me wished I could drift in the boat with my dad forever. That's how I wanted to remember him— *alive* and in my life—fishing, skiing, playing golf, pulling practical jokes, sharing books and writers and writing.

Though he'd had to travel to promote his books, my father had been a home-body at heart. Early morning and late night were when he did his writing. The rest of the day was for living, so that he'd have something to write about— that's what he used to say. And anyone who ever met him knew he meant it. My dad squeezed as much out of a day as a person possibly could. It wasn't so much that he was always on the go; it was just that he savored everything he did. For Dad, morning coffee on the deck was as special as a tropical cruise. And because he got such a kick out of everything, Mom and I did too.

You might say his way of looking at life was contagious.

I felt my throat tighten. But it hadn't been real. *He* hadn't been real! The life he'd lived with Mom and me was a huge lie—loving husband, devoted father—*all a lie!* He'd said so himself.

I thought of the note he left on the dresser. It was the shortest thing he'd ever written. But it was also the most powerful. Just three sentences.

Closets are horrible places—small, dark and crowded with secrets and lies. After a while you just can't seem to keep the door shut. I'm sorry.

Then he took a gun and blew his life to pieces. Mine too. With one little bullet, he managed to shatter his skull and turn me into a walking box of mismatched puzzle pieces. Nothing fit anymore.

Rage and frustration began to swirl inside me like a hurricane whipping itself into a frenzy. Faster and faster it whirled, slashing at my guts and slamming my heart into my ribs. I wanted to yell it out of me, but there were no words for what I was feeling. And besides, the person I needed to yell at wasn't there to hear me.

Why, Dad? Why did you dump this on me and then leave? I believed in you, but you lied to me. So now what am I supposed to think? What am I supposed to believe? You were gay, and you killed yourself. Should I hate you for that? Or am I supposed to feel sorry for you? You should have told me.

I picked up my pen and started to write.

Chapter Six

League volleyball started the next day.

The junior girls played first. After them it was the junior boys, then the varsity girls and finally us. With each match, the bleachers filled up a little more. By the time we took the court, the gym was packed.

The noise was incredible. We were playing Glenlawn—our longstanding rival according to Jai—so their fans were trying to out-scream ours. And just in case that wasn't enough to clean out a person's earwax, there were horns and kazoos and warm-up music bouncing off the walls too.

I was pumped, but because I was playing a new position, I was also a little nervous. In the past, I'd always been a weak side hitter, but Mr. Hudson said my long arms were great for blocking, so he'd switched me to middle.

His theory was put to the test on the very first rally. Glenlawn served a floater to the back line. *Bump*, *set*, *smash*—we returned it. But Glenlawn dug it up and their setter made a perfect pass over to power. The hitter took his approach and I slid toward Paul, who was playing weak side. As Glenlawn's hitter went up, so did Paul and I. *Slam!* The ball ricocheted off our arms, back onto the hitter and out of play. Point, Dakota.

The next three points went to Glenlawn. We took the two after that. And on it went—seesawing back and forth the whole match. No sooner would one team go on a run than the momentum would shift, and the other team would take the lead.

We won the first game. Glenlawn took the second. The third and deciding one went down to the wire, ending 23–21 in our favor.

Victory was sweet. Glenlawn left our gym vowing revenge.

Tess jumped down from the bleachers and ambushed me. She shoved a felt marker under my nose as if it were a microphone.

"Great game, Shaw," she said. Her expression was serious and her voice was deep and reporterish. "Sixteen big stops in today's match. Could you tell our listeners how it feels to be the Dakota Lancers' new blocking machine?"

I made a face and pushed the felt marker away. "You are too funny."

She giggled and gave me a hug. "I know. It was an awesome game though," she said. "And you did have some pretty amazing blocks. Why don't we grab a burger, and I can interview you for the paper. My treat," she sweetened the pot.

"You're buying?" I waggled my eyebrows at her. "Hey, guys!" I hollered. "Tess is gonna treat us to—" That's as far as I got before she stomped on my foot.

"Not the whole team!" she shushed me. "What do you take me for—the Bank of Canada?"

I laughed. It was so easy to rile Tess, sometimes I just couldn't resist. "Gotcha!" I said. Then I nodded toward the exit where my mom was standing.

Tess looked and waved, and my mom waved back.

"Thanks for the offer, Tess," I said, "but I can't tonight. I already have a date with another one of my fans."

Tess pretended to be miffed. "Fine. If that's the way you want it, I'll just have to feature some other lucky guy in my article. Have fun on your date." Then she waved at my mom again and took off across the gym in Jai's direction.

"Exciting game," Mom said as we walked out to the car. "I was on the edge of my seat the whole match." She wiped imaginary sweat from her forehead. "It's tough being a mother. I think I get as much of a workout as you do. My shoulders are still tight."

I held out my hand for the keys. "Then you better let me drive. We wouldn't want to have an accident."

Mom and I rehashed the game the whole way home—reliving the big kills and great plays, and agonizing over lost points and questionable calls. We were still on the subject long after we walked into our apartment.

"I am really glad I joined this team," I said, flopping down onto the couch. "The guys are great, and Mr. Hudson is a fantastic coach. I'm learning a lot. And I don't even mind the practices— not completely anyway."

Mom laughed. "Well, it certainly looks like they're paying off. The way you smash that ball, I sure as heck wouldn't want to be on the receiving end of it."

I shrugged. "If we don't hammer it down the opposition's throat, they'll pound it down ours. I just wish I could do it more consistently."

"You will," Mom said with the total confidence of someone who doesn't actually have to do the deed.

"But you know," I leaned back and put my feet up on the coffee table, "as much as I love to whale on that ball, I like blocking it even better. It's like I'm a brick wall or a force field or something. When the ball bounces off my arms and back at the hitter, I feel so pumped I swear I could jump right over that net. I just want to…" I noticed a faraway look take over my mom's face.

"Earth to Mom," I said.

Her eyes focused again. She gave her head a shake as if to clear it.

Then she said, "Did you know your dad used to play volleyball?"

I didn't answer. It had been a good evening. Why did Mom have to spoil it by bringing up Dad?

She kept on talking.

"Of course you know he played volleyball. You've heard his stories almost as many times as I have. The point is, blocking was his favorite part of the game too. He described the adrenaline rush he got from it exactly the same way you described it. He said he felt like he was going to fly over the net." She paused and waited for me to say something.

I didn't.

So she started up again. "Don't you think that's interesting?"

"Yeah, real interesting," I muttered, suddenly wanting out of the conversation. I pushed myself off the couch and headed for my room. "G'night."

"Shaw?" Mom called after me. "What's the matter?"

I didn't stop.

"Nothing," I said. "I'm just tired. G'night."

I knew it wasn't fair walking out on Mom like that. I also knew my dad wasn't going to clear out of my life just because I refused to talk about him.

What I didn't know was that Mom knew all that too.

Not five minutes after I shut my bedroom door, she was knocking on it.

"Shaw," she said, "may I come in? I have something you might be interested in."

My jaw tightened. I didn't want a repeat of the other night's yelling match.

"What?" I scowled, swinging open the door.

She laid a heavy leather-bound book in my hands.

"Your father's journal," she said quietly. She kissed my cheek. "Goodnight."

Chapter Seven

"I'm telling you, man—she likes you!"

Even though Jai was right in my face, he wasn't exactly whispering. I was pretty sure everyone on the bus heard him. The old lady across the aisle looked like she was waiting for me to answer.

"I like her too." I kept my voice low, hoping Jai would get the message. "We're friends."

Jai let out an exasperated sigh. "Not that kind of like, man. The girl/guy kind. You know."

"Is this just a feeling you have, or did she actually say something?"

"Well… not in so many words."

I shook my head. "There you—"

"She didn't have to!" Jai cut me off. "It's obvious."

"To someone with a runaway imagination maybe. Trust me," I said. "Tess does not have a crush on me—unless you count all the times she's clobbered me with her books."

"A clear demonstration of affection," Jai said smugly.

"Get out. You're crazy," I told him.

"No, I'm serious!"

"So am I." I jerked my thumb toward the window. "This is your stop. Get out."

As I watched Jai get off the bus, I thought about what he'd said. Tess and me?

Not likely. I'd walked on her feet and yelled in her face the very first day we'd met. Not the best technique for getting a girlfriend. It was only because we had English every day that she bothered to speak to me again at all. I mean, it's pretty hard to stay permanently mad at someone who sits right behind you. So little by little the iceberg between us had melted, and we'd become friends. *Friends!* That was all.

I dumped my books onto a chair and flopped full out across my bed. It had been a tough day, and I needed a breather before tackling my homework. I reached blindly for the new issue of *Sports Illustrated* on the headboard. But instead of the cool, slippery cover, my hand fell on the soft leather of my father's journal.

As if it had burned me, I pulled away and jumped off the bed. I stood there feeling stupid. Just grab the magazine, my brain said. But all I could do was stare at that journal.

For two days it had been sitting on my headboard, and for two days I had been avoiding it. I knew my mom had given it to me for a reason. I just wasn't sure I wanted to know what that reason was—especially if it meant uncovering more truths about my dad.

It's crazy the way a person's mind works. If my father had been killed in a plane crash, or if he'd died of a heart attack, he'd still be gone and I'd still have a gaping hole in my life. And that would be horrible. But he hadn't just died. He'd killed himself, and that made the situation a million times worse. His death wasn't just stealing from my future; it was stealing from my past too. He'd said his life was a lie. Did that mean his life with me was also a lie? And all the stuff we'd done together—was that phony too? Had it only been important to me? I had so many questions.

And no way to get the answers.

I continued to stare at the journal. Unless the answers were in there.

Tentatively, I picked up the book by the worn leather spine and sat back down on the bed. But several more minutes passed before I could actually bring myself to open it.

The journal spanned several years. From the lengthy gaps between entries, it was clear that my father had written in it only when he had something important to say. After just a few pages, I understood why my mother had given it to me. Raw with emotion, Dad's words leapt off the paper, attacking me with a fierceness that caught me off-guard. My dad was talking to me, and I had no choice but to listen.

With the turn of each page, I felt myself being pulled deeper and deeper into the journal.

An hour went by before I was able to find my way back to the surface. It was only then that I realized I'd been reading the same passage over and over.

I awoke with every intention of getting straight to work—in fact, I was anxious to start. For days I'd been struggling with a difficult scene, and though I had written it at least five different ways, I couldn't get it right. But during the night—while I thought I was sleeping—it finally sorted itself out. As I waited for the coffee to finish brewing, my fingers twitched to get at the keyboard.

But I didn't move fast enough, and by the time I finally poured my coffee, morning had started to scale the North

Shore mountains. Fascinated, I watched it inch its way up the far slope, pushing the night back to let streaks of pink and gold wash the sky. My gaze became fixed on the rocky ridge. I didn't want to blink for fear of missing the precise instant the sun broke over the summit. As if teasing me, it stopped and waited for me to look away so it might rush the sky undetected. But I was the patient one, and giving in at last, morning took the mountain—and me.

I knew my writing would have to wait. Morning had made such an effort to arrive, I had to go out and welcome it.

Watching Shaw sleep, I was both awed and envious. To be twelve again and know the serenity of an uncluttered mind! He looked so peaceful that I had second thoughts about waking him. Perhaps I should go alone. But then I decided—no. He could sleep any time.

This particular morning was only going to happen once.

There's wondrous magic in communing with nature while the rest of the world sleeps. It's an experience that can't be explained. If you're lucky enough to share it with someone special, it's even better.

Shaw and I silently slid the boat into the water and inhaled the morning before climbing aboard. In the distance, clumsy cormorants hung in the air above a school of fish, and we aimed the boat in their direction.

For a while the gulls followed us, circling and squawking overhead. But they soon realized we had nothing to give them and tired of our company.

We let our lines out and then proceeded to ignore them. The truth is we didn't really care about fishing; it just provided a respectable excuse to be on the water when all sane people were still asleep. It meant we didn't have to explain the perfection of the moment. It was ours alone.

I read the last sentence again. *It was ours alone.* Then I closed the journal and allowed crushing waves of joy and grief to wash over me.

Chapter Eight

Even though I'd only begun to read the journal, it had already shaken awake a part of me that had been asleep since my dad's death. For four months I'd been numb, and I hadn't even known it. Whenever I'd thought of my dad, his lifeless body was the only image I could conjure.

And now I knew why. As awful as that vision was, as angry as it made me,

I could handle it. It was the memory of my dad alive that started an ache I couldn't shut down.

As for the homosexuality thing, I didn't want to think about that at all. What guy does? Fags, queers, homos— those are perverts, not a guy's dad. Not *my* dad! He was a jock, women liked him—he was married, for Pete's sake! And he'd fathered a kid—me! He couldn't be gay. Could he?

The more I rolled the idea around in my head, the less sense it made. Why would my dad have married my mom if he'd been gay? Was he trying to fool people into thinking he was straight? I thought about my parents. They couldn't have faked being happy for twenty years. Their marriage had to have been real.

Which brought me back to my original question. How could my dad have been gay?

Then I had an unnerving thought. What if he hadn't known he was gay until *after* he got married? Was that possible? And if it was, then was it also possible that I might be *that way* too? Could it be genetic? I was pretty sure I wasn't attracted to guys. Maybe that could change.

I didn't like this at all. And it wasn't the sort of thing I could talk over with my friends.

Suddenly, I thought of Tess. *She likes you*, Jai had said. Of course, that had made me wonder if I liked her back. Tess was pretty and fun and smart. What was there not to like? But we were just friends. That's what I'd told Jai. Under the circumstances, I decided that was probably a good way to keep it.

The newspaper club had a table set up outside the gym. I grabbed a paper on the way by and stuffed it inside my books. Somewhere between chemistry and English, I'd have to find a couple of minutes to read it—the articles Tess had written, at any rate. She was bound to ask me about them.

I finished my chemistry assignment before the period was over and managed to read the entire paper. I have to say that Tess's writing was pretty good. That unmistakable energy of hers came through loud and clear, and she took an original approach to her subjects.

The rest of the paper was junk.

One article in particular really bugged me. Some guy named Roy Ranier raged on for three-quarters of a page about the unfair amount of recognition sports got compared with other programs such as art, drama and music. The article was just one long, pathetic whine, and it really ticked me off. I was still fuming about it when I got to English.

So when Tess asked me how I liked the paper, my answer probably wasn't as tactful as it could have been.

"Except for the stuff you wrote, it sucked," I said.

You would have thought I'd uncorked a bottle and spit on the genie who'd been locked up inside for a thousand years. Tess was in my face so fast I could count the freckles on her nose.

"What! How can you say that? It does not! Did you even bother to read it?" She stormed.

"Yes, I read it," I replied calmly, "and most of it was pretty lame. Sorry." I shrugged. "But you asked."

She planted her fists on her hips and glared at me harder than ever. "Like what, for instance?"

"Tess," I tried to defuse the situation before it got out of hand, "it doesn't matter. I shouldn't have said anything. It's just my opinion anyway."

But Tess was already too mad to back down. "You can't just go flinging insults around, you know!" she huffed. "Put your money where your mouth is. If you're going to criticize, you better have something to back it up!"

I slammed my books onto my desk and dug out the paper. "Fine." I glared back at her. "You want proof? Try this." Then I shoved Roy Ranier's article under her nose.

"What's the matter with this?" she demanded.

"What's not the matter with it?"

"Get real, Shaw! This is a very important issue. I can't believe you don't see that. Just because you're a jock, it doesn't mean everyone is. Those other programs are worthwhile too, and they deserve a lot more support than they get! And I don't just mean money. I'm talking morale, promotion, positive reinforcement. It isn't just athletes who deserve recognition, you know. Everybody who—"

"I agree," I said, cutting her off.

Tess looked surprised. "You do?"

I nodded. "Of course."

Her eyes narrowed suspiciously. "Then what's your problem?" She smacked her hand on the paper. "That's exactly what this article is all about."

I shook my head. "No, it isn't. *That's* the problem. Instead of setting out arguments and solutions, Ranier has sniveled his way through the subject. He hasn't helped the cause; he's hurt it. He should have presented music, art and drama on a par with athletics. He should have suggested ways of serving everybody. Then people would pay attention. But instead, he used all this ink to whine. Nobody's gonna listen to that."

I knew Tess was going to fly back with another argument in old Roy's defense, but there was a split second where she seemed off-balance. I was pretty sure I'd made my point. But then Miss Boswell arrived and called the class to order.

"Well, if you have all the answers, maybe *you* should have written the article," Tess muttered as she threw herself into her seat.

Miss Boswell perched on the edge of her desk and waited for the class to settle down. She had a bunch of papers in her hand.

"Your last writing assignment," she said, waving them at us. Then she smiled. "For the most part, they're pretty good. You're all making progress. The descriptions are becoming more vivid, and the narrative is generally crisper. I've made specific comments and suggestions on each of your papers. Before I hand them back, I'd like to read one aloud as an example of how, as writers, we can really get inside a topic. Listen up."

It was June 4, the sky was blue, and classes had let out early. What more could a sixteen-year-old guy ask for? I shed the school like an unwanted jacket and started to jog home. I felt my pocket for my essay. It was still there. I smiled, thinking of the 'A' on the top of the paper, and my teacher's "Your best work yet!" scrawled beside it. I couldn't wait for my dad to see it.

The thing is—he never did.

As Miss Boswell read, I stared at my desktop. I knew the other kids were looking around the classroom trying to figure out whose paper she was reading, but amazingly, I didn't care. That struck me as strange. A few weeks ago I'd panicked at the mere thought of anyone finding out about my dad. It was as if putting my feelings into words had set me free, and it was a relief not to have to hide anymore.

When Miss Boswell started handing back our essays, Tess turned around. I steeled myself for her to start ranting again. All she said was, "Like I said—maybe *you* should have written the article."

Chapter Nine

As we dropped back to the baseline and waited for the referee's signal to change sides, Jai and I blinked at each other in disbelief.

Our team had just been smoked. All we'd managed in the entire game were two lousy points. And the team that beat us wasn't even ranked! At least they hadn't been—though that was probably going to change after the tournament. One game away from the playoff round and they were still undefeated.

The referee blew his whistle and we jogged around to the other side of the court and took our positions.

I raised my hands and faced the net. From the other side, my opponent leered back at me. He was so close I could feel his breath on my skin. I could smell it too. He reeked of onions. I tensed my nostrils and tried to concentrate on the game.

The whistle blew again, and the other team sent a floater to the back of our court. We returned it, but the ball nicked the net on the way over, and the opposition dug it up easily and drove it back. Jai tried to save it, but he never had a chance.

"Point," the referee said, and we got set for the next serve.

Onion Breath was in my face again.

"Maybe you should just concede and let the bleeding stop," he jeered. "You're only gonna get killed."

"The only thing that's gonna kill us is your breath," I muttered back. "Ever hear of mouthwash?"

Then the ball was in play again. It was a long rally, the kind that could swing the momentum in our favor if we won the point. We didn't.

"What a bunch of losers," Onion Breath sneered as we took our places at the net once more. "Especially your runt of a setter. Where'd you pick him up? At a refugee garage sale? What's the matter—no white kids go to your school?"

At first I thought I must have been hearing things. But when the look on Onion Breath's face became smugger than ever, I realized my hearing was just fine. If the ball hadn't been served then, I would have punched him in the mouth.

I tried to concentrate on the game, but part of me was thinking about how he'd insulted Jai. The more I thought about it, the madder I got. By the time the play had gone back and forth a couple of times, I was steaming. The other team hit the ball hard and deep, but Brian dug it up and passed it to Jai, and he made a great set—to me.

As I took my approach, I could see Onion Breath getting ready to block me. The part of me that was still thinking about the game considered dinking the ball past him for the sure point. But the part of me that was boiling mad needed to pound that ball with every ounce of strength in my body. Conscious of Onion Breath mirroring my moves on the other side of the net, I faked my jump, sending him into the air a split second before me. When I went up, he was already on his way back to the floor. Reaching all the way to my shoes, I laid into the ball with everything I had and slammed it straight down. Right into his face.

We lost the match, but seeing the red imprint of the ball on Onion Breath's forehead for the rest of the game helped soothe the disappointment a little. I'd made my point, and there were no more insults.

At least not during the game. After the tournament it was a different story.

As usual, Jai took forever to change, so by the time he was finally ready to go, the rest of our team had left.

Onion Breath hadn't. He and four of his friends were waiting in the parking lot. I figured they'd glare at us and take cheap shots from a distance, but I was wrong. They cut us off before we got to the car.

Right away Onion Breath started in on Jai, pushing him and making racist remarks. Jai did his best to shrug free and keep heading for the car, but he was definitely outsized. Onion Breath's friends soon had him surrounded.

I started to move to Jai's defense, but two of them cut me off.

"What's the matter? Your little ragtop friend need a babysitter?" one of them said in a singsong voice.

Onion Breath turned his attention from Jai to me. He took the volleyball he'd been holding under his arm and bounced it off my head—once, twice, three times. When I didn't react, he got right in my face and sneered, "Where's your smart mouth now, Paki-lover? Now that the net's gone, you're not quite so brave." Then, with a cocky smile, he threw the volleyball at my head again.

"Maybe not," I said, catching it. "But you still stink, and you're still a jerk."

Then I whipped the ball back and caught him right between the eyes.

Onion Breath totally lost it and charged me like a tackle for the Green Bay Packers. We both went sprawling. I took a couple of blows to the head before I realized I was in a fight. But then I landed a shot to his gut, and the air rushed out of him like he was a popped balloon.

The next thing I knew, we were being yanked apart and dragged to our feet by a couple of teachers. But instead of hauling us back into the school like I expected, they simply lectured us for a few minutes and sent us on our way.

"Nice eye," Tess said when I showed up at school on Monday.

I smirked. "You should see the other guy."

Tess snorted. "I've heard that before. What happened?"

So I told her.

"What a bunch of losers," she said when I'd finished.

"No kidding," I agreed. "There's probably not a nicer guy than Jai in all of Winnipeg! Why pick on him?"

She shrugged. "Simple. He's East Indian. Idiots like Onion Breath and his friends don't care how great a human being he is. All they know is that he's different. They're prejudiced, and they probably don't even know why. No doubt they get it from their parents. I mean, hatred isn't a quality you're born with. It's something that's learned."

"That's pathetic!"

"Of course it is," Tess said calmly. "But it's not going to change unless we do something about it."

I touched my black eye. "I already did."

She shook her head. "That's not what I mean." Then her eyes gleamed mischievously. "Haven't you heard? The pen is mightier than the sword."

Chapter Ten

I expected Jai to be as upset about Onion
Breath and his pals as I was. After all,
he was the one they'd been picking on.
But the incident didn't seem to faze him.
Once it was over—it was over. He never
mentioned it again.

So I didn't either.

After volleyball practice on Monday,
Jai was standing in the middle of the

court, staring up at the walls of the gym.

"What are you doing?" I said.

He grinned at me. "Just trying to figure out where we should hang our next championship banner."

I rolled my eyes. "Aren't you getting ahead of yourself just a little? Provincials are still a long way off. Considering how we played in that last tournament, we may not even get that far."

Jai waved off my concerns. "No problem. We're getting better all the time. As long as we win our conference, we're in. The way I see it, we—"

"Hey!" Brian poked his head out of the change room. Everybody's going over to Dale's to watch a video and order pizza. You guys coming?"

Jai immediately started jogging across the gym. I shook my head. "Nah. I can't. I have a ton of homework."

It was the truth, and though some of my assignments weren't due for a while, I was determined to get them out of the way.

I headed for my books the second I got home. I didn't even make a pit stop at the fridge. But as soon as I saw my dad's journal sitting on the headboard, my willpower took a nosedive.

There was something magnetic about that journal. It was so emotionally exhausting that I could never read more than one or two entries at a time, but as soon as I'd digested them, I was ready for more.

I tried to wrench my gaze away, but it was no use.

Just one entry! I told myself sternly, picking up the journal and opening it to where I'd left off. I flopped onto my bed and wadded a pillow behind my head. *Just one entry!*

That was my last thought before the words on the page swallowed me up and transported me back in time.

Mostly my dad had been a novelist, but every now and then he'd tried his hand at something else. *Foggy Friday* was one of those something elses. It was a play—a farce that he'd whipped up between books— just for fun. Therefore it was a major surprise when a theatre company in Toronto decided to produce it. Dad said he'd always wanted to do the playwright-on-opening-night shtick, so when the company invited him to attend the premiere, he jumped at the chance. Naturally Mom and I went along too.

It was great! Dad gave us the royal tour of Toronto, and we even took in a Blue Jays' game. But the best part was the play itself.

As I gobbled up the journal description of the crazy events preceding the performance, I found myself smirking.

The curtain had been scheduled to go up at eight. We were going to hit the hotel lounge for pre-performance toasts, take in the play and have a celebration dinner afterwards. But no sooner had Dad told us the plan than there was a knock at the door. Then a troupe of strange-looking people swooped into our suite, toting a bunch of boxes and pushing a clothes rack dripping in glitter.

The next thing I knew, I was being whisked into another room and relieved of my clothes. Normally I wouldn't give up my jeans without a fight, but the huge grin on my dad's face as he lost his own pants made me suspect he might have had a hand in this takeover. And since he'd never sold me out in the past, I let myself be abducted.

In twenty minutes it was over, and I was back in the main room, smelling like an ad for men's cologne and looking like a Liberace wannabe in a silver-sequined tux and black patent leather shoes.

And then I saw my parents. At least I think they were my parents, though the resemblance was minimal. Dad was wearing a black satin tux with tails. It might have been elegant if it weren't for the gold bowtie, cummerbund, gloves and shoes. Even his top hat and walking stick were gold.

But it was Mom who really took the cake. She looked as if she'd escaped from an old movie. From the sequined cloche covering her hair to the three-inch heels on her feet, she was dressed completely in red. Even the feather boa trailing behind her and the cigarette holder dangling from her fingers were red.

A long-sleeved dress hugged her like a shimmering snakeskin and puddled on the floor at her feet. Her fingers, wrists and throat sparkled with jewels. My jaw dropped. *This was my mother?*

Then she pursed scarlet lips into a pout and batted two-inch eyelashes at my dad. And that's when we all cracked up.

At the theatre, cameras snapped our picture every time we turned around. In fact, everywhere we went that night, people's eyes bugged out, but we didn't care. We were having too much fun.

I put aside the journal and bounced off the bed.

"Mom," I hollered, tearing down the hall and into the living room. "Where's the photo album?"

She looked up from her book.

"In the chest at the foot of my bed. Why? What are you looking for?"

I didn't bother answering. I just took off for her bedroom. That's where she found me fifteen minutes later, cross-legged on the carpet, my nose buried in the album.

"Do you remember this?" I said, pointing to a picture of us in our *Foggy Friday* opening-night glitz.

"Oh my god," she murmured, dropping down beside me. She started to chuckle. "Look at the three of us. What a bunch of hams! Trust your father to come up with that kind of a stunt. The costumes, the hairdresser, the make-up artist—it must have cost him a small fortune." Then she laughed again. "But it sure was a hoot."

She flipped the page. "And this was that summer we rented a houseboat in the Okanagan. Do you remember?"

"Sure do." I grinned. "I snapped this one right before Dad threw you into the lake."

She peered at the picture more closely. "You know, I think you're right."

Then she grinned too. "But that's okay. I got even with him. When he asked for a beer, he should have made it clear that he wanted to drink it—not wear it."

For more than an hour, we pored over the album, reliving the moments captured in the photographs. Each one brought back treasured memories.

"Were we really as happy as we look in the pictures?" I asked.

Mom eyed me curiously. "Don't you remember?"

I shrugged uncomfortably. "Yes and no. I thought I was happy, but after... after what Dad did..."

"You mean his suicide?"

I frowned and continued more quietly, "Yeah. After his suicide, I wasn't sure if my memories were real. I didn't know—"

She squeezed my hand. "What you remember is how it was. Every minute was absolutely real." She smiled. "Don't doubt that for a second."

Most of me believed her, but there was still that particle of doubt. How could she be so sure? "But Dad...he... he wasn't who we thought he was. He was...he was...gay." There, I'd said it.

Mom smiled sadly. "Yes, he was."

"So how could he...how could you... why did you guys..." I couldn't seem to get the words out. "Did you know?" I finally blurted.

Mom smiled again and nodded.

"Of course I knew. Your father never told me, but he didn't have to. You don't share a bed with someone for twenty years and not know something like that. Still, I wish he'd felt he could have told me about it. We shared just about every-thing, but that was the one subject that was taboo. I tried to bring it up once, but the look of terror that came into his eyes made me back off. You see, Shaw, your father couldn't acknowledge his sexuality even to himself. When he was growing up, things weren't open like they are now. No matter how hard he tried, he couldn't shake the guilt. In his own eyes, he was a monster. How could he expect others to accept him?"

She squeezed my hand again.

"But that doesn't change the life we shared. It was every bit as wonderful as it looks in the photographs. I couldn't have had a better husband, and you couldn't have had a better dad. Dylan Sebring was the finest man I have ever known. I truly loved him, and I shall miss him always."

Chapter Eleven

As I got deeper into my father's journal, I noticed a change in the writing. The joy of living that had filled most of the earlier entries gave way to a kind of restlessness that caromed from one topic to the next. It was as if my dad was playing tag with himself, and he was always "it." He complained about the unfair expectations of editors and publishers.

He worried that his creativity was drying up. He despaired over the ecological state of the planet.

But as I read each rant, I had the uneasy feeling that these weren't really the things that were bothering him. Something else—something he wasn't saying—was at the bottom of his agitation.

Then I got to that last entry. And though it answered my questions and silenced my doubts, I wish I'd never read it. Even more, I wish my dad had never written it.

It was a declaration of surrender. My father was finished fighting. Overpowered by demons that had plagued him his whole life, he was finally admitting defeat. It was all on those last pages—and I felt his despair as surely as if it was my own.

The immense weight of his burden almost crushed me. And yet my father had carried it around for a lifetime without anyone even suspecting. I hadn't known about his confusion and anger, his feelings of failure, his self-loathing and guilt. I hadn't had any idea of the constant fear he lived with. The worry that his secret would one day be found out, and when it was—his life, Mom's, mine, and ours as a family would be ruined.

And so he'd killed himself.

I slammed shut the journal and began pacing.

I was angry and frustrated, and I needed to hit something. My father's death had been so senseless. So wrong!

Dylan Sebring had been a wonderful, caring human being. But he'd hated himself because he wasn't normal. Normal. *Normal!* What the heck was *normal*? And who got to decide that? Bigots like Onion Breath?

I thought of Jai. In a way, he was caught in the same trap as my dad.

No matter what he did, he couldn't change the color of his skin, and according to some people, that automatically made him less of a person.

It wasn't as if this was the first time I'd ever thought about prejudice. But it was the first time that I understood how devastating it was to be on the receiving end of it. Just for being different.

It was Friday and school had just let out. Tess, Jai and I were heading for the bus stop.

"Are you guys going to the dance next week?" Tess asked.

"They don't call me Twinkle-Toes for nothing." Jai grinned, breaking into something that looked like a disco-variety highland fling.

"Right." Tess eyed him warily and then turned to me. "What about you, Shaw?"

Behind her, Jai was grinning and nodding like one of those wobbly-headed dogs people put in the back window of their cars. I tried to ignore him, but it was pretty much impossible, and it wasn't long before Tess swiveled around to see what he was doing. He instantly started dancing again.

"Don't mind me," he said. "I'm just practicing my moves."

Tess shook her head. "Whatever." She turned back to me. "Are *you* going to the dance?"

"I'm not really much of a dancer," I said.

Behind Tess, Jai grimaced and began shaking his head like crazy. Obviously, he didn't like my answer.

I pretended not to notice. But when Tess didn't say anything, I started to feel guilty.

"Are you going?" I said to fill the silence.

She shrugged. "Maybe. It depends."

"On what?"

"On who else is going, for one thing. And the newspaper, for another. It comes out next Friday, which means I could be up all Thursday night, making sure it's ready. I might be totally wiped. I guess I'll have to wait and see."

"Yeah, me too," I said. I glanced at Jai. He was all smiles.

It was the first free weekend I'd had since school had started—no volleyball and no homework—so I should have felt great. But I didn't. There were a million thoughts tearing around inside my head, and I couldn't seem to sort them out.

"Would you please sit down," Mom complained, whipping a cushion at me. "You're driving me nuts!"

"I can't." I chucked the cushion back and took another lap around the living room. "I'm restless."

"Who would've guessed?" Mom said sarcastically.

"Why don't you go for a run?"

"That won't help."

Mom headed for the coat cupboard and grabbed her jacket. "I have to pick up a few things at the drugstore. Why don't you come with me? The walk will do you good."

I shook my head.

"Suit yourself," she sighed. As she let herself out the door she added, "But try not to wear a hole in the carpet, okay?"

After she'd gone, I paced a bit more and then threw myself down onto the couch. Maybe television would distract me. I flipped through the channels a few times, but nothing held my attention. I turned the set off and picked up the newspaper instead. I must have stared at the same headline for two minutes. My eyes were reading the words, but for some reason they weren't getting to my brain.

Well, maybe they were, but my brain was too busy to notice. Dad, Jai, volleyball, Tess, Dad, Tess—my thoughts ricocheted back and forth so fast it felt like a racquetball game was being played in my head. What I needed was a way to untangle my thoughts and look at them one at a time.

Write them down.

Of course! Why hadn't I thought of that before? It had always worked for my dad.

Suddenly I could see him sitting at his desk. Normally he worked at the computer, but whenever he was starting something new, he liked to work directly on paper. For a while he'd just hold his pen and stare into space. Eventually, though, his eyes would glaze over. He'd reach for an old baseball he used as a paperweight, and rolling the ball absently in his free hand, he would begin to write.

I got some paper and set it out on the table.

Then I sat down and picked up my pen. But ten minutes later, I still hadn't written anything. I got up again and walked down the hall to my mother's bedroom and opened the chest at the foot of her bed.

I'm not sure how long Mom had been home before I realized she'd come in. Something made me look up from my writing. I saw her standing in the entrance to the dining room. She was staring at the ball in my hand. And she was smiling.

Chapter Twelve

On Friday, Mr. Hudson called a lunch-time volleyball meeting to talk about the playoffs. It suddenly dawned on me that the season was nearly over. For a second I almost panicked. During the last couple of months—while I'd been trying to sort out my life—volleyball had kept me afloat like a life preserver. And though I knew I didn't need it anymore, I also knew that after it was over, I was going to have a big chunk of time to fill.

The bell rang for afternoon classes, and I took off for the main hall.

"Where's the fire?" Jai demanded. "Or are you just anxious to get to math?"

"I want to pick up a newspaper," I explained.

"It's not like there's only one copy," he pointed out as he hurried to keep up.

"I know, but—"

"Great article, Shaw," someone said.

"Good one," somebody else called from down the hall and gave me a thumbs-up.

"Thanks," I called back, working hard to keep the smile on my face from turning into a Jai-sized grin.

Jai grabbed my arm. "Hold on. Am I hearing right? *You* wrote an article for the paper?"

I nodded.

"Are you serious?" When I nodded again he said, "I didn't know you could write your name—never mind a whole article! You've been holding out on me, man."

He punched me in the shoulder and tore off down the hall. By the time I caught up with him, he had his nose buried in a newspaper.

I felt like a celebrity. It seemed as if everyone in the school had read my article, and at each class change they stopped me in the hall to comment on it. My last subject was English, and when I got to the room, Tess was standing outside the door waiting for me.

I waved and started to cut across the traffic, but a tall, blond guy with glasses and a skimpy goatee cut me off. Before I knew what was happening, he grabbed hold of my hand and started shaking the life out of it.

"Excellent article, Shaw," he said, his rubbery red lips giving way to a mouthful of braces. "If that doesn't wake up the social consciences of people, I don't know what will. I hope you'll be doing more articles for us in the future." Then he gave me back my hand and continued on his way.

Scratching my head, I walked over to Tess.

I jerked a thumb in the direction of the blond kid's retreating back. "Do more articles for *us*?" I said. "What's that supposed to mean? I've never seen that guy before in my life. Who is he?"

Tess started to chuckle. "That guy," she said, "is Roy Ranier."

I shook my head. "Sorry, the name doesn't ring any bells."

Tess raised an eyebrow. "Well, it should. He's the one who wrote that article you hated so much. You know—

the one about sports versus other school programs?"

"That was him?" I said in disbelief.

"Uh-huh." Tess nodded and started into the room. "That was him. Obviously not how you expected your boss to look."

I followed her through the door. "My *boss*? What are you talking about?"

Though I couldn't see Tess's face, I could hear the smile in her voice. "Didn't you know? Roy is the editor of the paper."

I couldn't wait for Mom to get home from work. I was dying to show her the article.

"Well, what do you think?" I said when she'd finished it.

She read the headline out loud. "P is for People—not Prejudice." Then she looked across the table at me, and there was a gleam in her eye. "You don't pull any punches, do you?"

I sat forward in my chair. "Not if I can help it. It's time the subject was brought out into the open."

"Well, you've certainly done that, all right. This is heavy-duty journalism, Shaw—and powerfully written. It's not the sort of piece that is going to be easy to ignore. I wouldn't be the least bit surprised if there are some far-reaching effects from it."

I couldn't help grinning. "Good. I want to wake people up." I leaned across the table excitedly. "And I already have an idea for a follow-up article, focusing on the positive side of the issue. You know—so kids will know there are things they can do to make a difference. I thought that if I—"

Mom didn't wait for me to finish. She stood up, came around the table and planted a kiss on the top of my head.

"What's that for?" I said, looking up.

"For being you," she replied. Then giving my shoulder a squeeze, she headed for the hall. "Wait here," she said. "I'll be right back."

When she returned, she had a folder full of papers. She plunked it on the table and sat back down in her chair.

I eyed the folder curiously. "What's that?"

Mom smiled. "It's something your father left. I've just been waiting for the right moment to give it to you."

"What is it?"

She pushed the folder towards me and smiled. "I think you'll know," she said. And then she got up and left the room.

For several minutes I just stared at the folder. There was no label or writing on the outside to indicate what was in it, but that was okay. Part of me wasn't ready to know anyway. That folder was a gift from my dad, and staring at it was like shaking a Christmas present. Until I looked inside the cover, it could be anything I wanted it to be.

But even a Christmas gift has to get unwrapped sometime. I opened the folder. Right away I knew what I was looking at.

It was a manuscript—well, part of one anyway. As I gaped at the title page, my throat became tight and my breathing quickened. I couldn't tear my eyes away from the title.

THE ROAD NOT TAKEN by Dylan and Shaw Sebring.

It was the beginning of the novel Dad and I had planned to write. I flipped through the pages excitedly. The outline, the summary, bits of narrative, descriptions, notes—random and incomplete for sure, but just like we'd talked about. Dad had made a start on our novel.

I stopped shuffling through the pages and took a deep breath.

And now it was up to me to finish it.

I didn't realize the phone had rung until Mom came into the dining room and handed it to me.

"Hello?" I said into the receiver.

"Hi, Shaw. It's Tess."

"Oh, hi," I said, coming back to reality. "What's up?"

"Well, to tell you the truth, I was just getting ready to leave for the dance. I was wondering if you were going."

I opened my mouth to answer, but she rushed on before I had the chance.

"I know you said you weren't a very good dancer, but if you want to learn, I'd be happy to teach you."

My heart sped up a little. I was glad Tess couldn't see the silly grin on my face.

"When you're finished with me, will I be able to move like Jai?" I said.

She gasped. "God, I hope not!"

I laughed. "In that case, count me in."

After I got off the phone, I put the pieces of the novel back into the folder. With a satisfying sense of purpose I marched down the hall to my room and plunked it on the headboard. Tomorrow I would write.

Then I opened my closet door and started searching for my blue shirt. Tonight I was going dancing.

Author's Note

This novel is a work of fiction, with two notable exceptions.

Firstly, Dakota Collegiate Institute is an actual high school in Winnipeg, Manitoba, though—to my knowledge—it doesn't publish a school newspaper. And secondly, Phil Hudson really is a teacher and the volleyball coach there. His wizardry with his teams is admired throughout the province and will undoubtedly make him a school legend forever.

The following is an excerpt from
another exciting Orca Soundings novel,
Zee's Way by Kristin Butcher.

Zee's Way

orca soundings

Kristin Butcher

Chapter One

I pushed open the bedroom window and stuck my head into the night. The rain had stopped right on schedule, and the clouds that had brought it were already scudding away. It had been like that all summer—hot sunny days, humid evenings and then—just after midnight—an hour of rain. Perfect conditions for a war.

Not that I wanted a war. None of the guys did. All we were after was a place to hang out. It was the merchants at Fairhaven Shopping Center who were looking for a fight.

As I stuffed the last of the cans into my pack, I thought back to the day Horace and I had visited the half-built mall. In an old neighborhood like ours, any kind of construction was worth checking out, but the guys and I had a real stake in this development. Before the dozers had come in and leveled everything, it had been our hangout. Maybe only an abandoned warehouse and parking lot to everybody else, but for us it was a place to chill. We could skateboard there, toss a baseball, kick a soccer ball or just get out of the rain.

At first we were super-ticked at being evicted, but after we got over the initial shock, we started thinking a shopping center might be just as good—

even better if it meant an arcade or a fast-food joint. The thing is, we never got to find out. Two minutes after we stepped onto the site, some lunatic came after us with a crowbar.

For what? All we were doing was having a look around. Since when was that a crime?

"Don't get all bent out of shape about it," my dad said when I told him what had happened. "That shopping strip has been financed by the businesses moving into it. Those merchants are just protecting their investment."

I shook my head and walked away. I should have known my dad would take their side.

I zipped my backpack and slung it over my shoulder. Then I boosted myself onto the window ledge, swung my legs over the sill and dropped to the ground. Staying in the shadows, I peered at the old, shingled houses crowding the street.

If any of the neighbors saw me taking a midnight stroll, my dad would know about it before breakfast. Then I'd have some explaining to do. But aside from the streetlamps, Barrett Avenue was dark. Mrs. Lironi's living room light was on, but that didn't mean she was up. She just kept the light on to discourage burglars. Everyone knew that—even the burglars.

I jogged across the yard and hurdled the hedge. My shadow stretched along the road beside me, bent arthritically where it climbed the curb. From the corner of my eye, I could see it matching my pace, and I was grateful for the company. I ran past a soggy flyer plastered to the sidewalk. It reminded me of the one the shopping center had put out for its grand opening.

That had been a huge event. Everyone in the neighborhood had come out for the bargains. Two for one at Oscar's Video Emporium, no GST at The Loonie Bin and 25 percent off all prescriptions at Fairhaven Drugs. Mario's Coffee Bar was selling large cappuccinos for the price of small ones, and there were free deli samples at Jackman's Market.

There was stuff going on in the parking lot too. Barbecues were sizzling up hot dogs and hamburgers. A clown with size thirty shoes was making balloon animals. Another one was painting faces. There was even a marching band. The local radio station was there too.

The guys and I showed up around one o'clock. By that time the place was so packed we could barely move. I squinted up at the white banner stretched across the storefronts. *Fairhaven Shopping Center—Grand Opening! Something for Everyone*, it said in huge blue letters.

But the second we arrived, the party was over. Oh, the festivities didn't stop; we just weren't allowed to be part of them.

It was discrimination, plain and simple. Not that the merchants came right out and told us to get lost. They just acted like we weren't there. Except when they thought we weren't looking. Then they couldn't stop staring.

Okay, so the five of us don't exactly blend into a crowd. Danny's got blue hair and Horace's head is shaved. Benny's lip is pierced, Mike has a thing for leather and studs, and we all have tattoos. So what! If our money's good, it shouldn't matter what we look like.

Try telling that to the Fairhaven merchants. Their minds were made up. They didn't want us around—not that first day or any day after that.

Whenever we'd go into a store, someone would follow us. Don't handle

the merchandise. Don't read the magazines. Don't block the aisles. It was
a song that played just for us. Women
pushing strollers could jam the aisles.
Old people could pick up the merchandise. Middle-aged men could browse the
magazines. It was just fifteen-year-old
guys who weren't allowed.

It was the same thing outside the
stores. All we had to do was stand on
the walkway in front of a shop and the
owner would glare at us until we moved
on. We couldn't even skateboard through
the parking lot without getting yelled at.
But since we had nowhere else to go, we
put up with it.

Until the No Loitering signs went
up. That's when we decided it was time
to take a stand. Not that we really did
anything different than what we were
already doing. We just did more of it.
And we did it on purpose.

Except for breaking the window in Jackman's Market. That was a total accident.

It was a Sunday morning. The shopping center wasn't open yet, so we were using the parking lot as a soccer field. The problem was that Benny didn't know his own strength. Before any of us realized what had happened, he'd kicked the ball through Jackman's window and set off the alarm.

We didn't wait around for the police. Accident or not, we knew we'd be blamed. And we were right. The store owners said the soccer ball was all the proof they needed. From then on they treated us like criminals. We were only allowed in a store two at a time—and only for five minutes. When we came out, we had to clear off the property completely. If we stood around for even thirty seconds, a police cruiser would show up.

I looked at the sky. The clouds were completely gone now, and I could see the glow of the shopping center lights ahead.

On the corner of Madison and Harper, I pressed close to a big oak tree and peered up and down the deserted street. Then when I was sure the coast was clear, I bolted across the road.

Feniuk's Hardware was the last store on the strip. There was nothing between it and the sidewalk except a Dumpster. I ducked behind the Dumpster and gazed up at the wall of the store. Bathed in the light of a nearby streetlamp, it was embarrassingly white and empty.

I pulled one of the spray cans from my backpack and began shaking it. Then I looked at the wall again.

It wouldn't be empty for long.